Annabelle

and the

Fairy Hunter

Forgotten Fairies Series

Book 1: *Annabelle, the Reluctant Fart Fairy*

Book 2: *Annabelle and the Fairy Hunter*

Forgotten Fairies Coloring Book

Also by M.T. Lott

Diary of a Farting Ghast (unofficial Minecraft diary)

Diary of a Farting Villager (unofficial Minecraft book)

Farting Animals Coloring Book

Super Cute Farting Animals Coloring Book

Farting Magical Creatures Coloring Book

Forgotten Fairies Series, Book Two

Annabelle

and the

Fairy Hunter

By,

M.T. Lott

To the true believers.

TABLE OF CONTENTS

Chapter One: The Gift

"HAPPY BIRTHDAY, ANNABELLE," everyone shouted as I blew out the candles on my strawberry pie. I was turning 505 years old. Fairies live so long that they only celebrate their birthdays every five years.

"Thank you, everyone," I said, beaming. It had been five years since the Queen made me a fart fairy at the Great Selecting. And, even though my fart fairy knowledge had helped save the world from a gigantic asteroid, I still was not very happy being a fart fairy.

But, I didn't want to think about that now. All of my family and friends were here to help celebrate my first birthday since I turned 500 years old and became a real, grown up fairy.

My old friends Sadie, Cynthia and Jane were here.

Jane, a rose fairy, brought several bunches of roses to decorate the party. Sadie, a daffodil fairy, brought a few pots with tiny daffodils blooming in them. Cynthia, a citrus fairy, brought fresh-squeezed orange juice for everyone to drink.

Some of my new friends were at the party too. They were part of the Forgotten Fairies Club I had helped start back when I first became a fart fairy and was looking to make friends with other fairies who had been assigned disgusting, thankless jobs.

Bob, the Black Widow fairy, was there, sitting in a corner, trying to stay out of any bright lights. Reggie, a flea fairy, was bouncing around with excitement, his tremendous height and bulk shaking the ground each time he landed. Rosalina, the snot fairy, was sitting patiently waiting for her slice of strawberry pie.

And, of course, my mom, my dad and my brother, Fevrile, were there too. Fevrile and I were twins, but he had his birthday party yesterday. My parents always had separate birthday parties for us so that we could each have our own special day.

After I blew out the candles, we all had slices of pie and sipped orange juice and talked for a while. Eventually, we came to my favorite part: Opening my presents!

I got some cool stuff. Mainly clothes and
jewelry, and Bob gave me a charm bracelet
with six different venomous spiders on it. It
was really awesome, but I saw my mom smirk
at it disapprovingly. Of course, I put it on my
wrist right away.

Finally, it was time to open Fevrile's
present. It was tradition that I opened his
present last, just like he opened my present
last. I got him a biography of Ignis Stultus, the
most famous fever fairy who ever lived. He
was excited.

"Here's my present," said Fevrile, handing
me a surprisingly well-wrapped box.

I undid the thick, red ribbon and ripped
open the glittery wrapping paper. Inside was a
plain cardboard box. I opened the box and
pulled out an old glass jar. It looked like

something made a few hundred years ago. I was not exactly sure what to make of the gift.

"Um, cool, Fevrile. Thanks. An old . . . uh, jar?"

Fevrile was grinning from ear-to-ear like a maniac. "Not just any old jar. Open it up."

I looked at the jar. It was completely empty. "What is this? A trick?" I asked suspiciously.

"Just open it. It is awesome," he said, shifting excitedly back and forth in his chair.

I looked around at all of my friends. They were completely clueless too. But, I could tell they wanted to know what was going to happen when I opened it.

When I opened it, nothing happened. I shook the jar a bit and put my eyeball up to the top and looked inside. "What is this, Fevrile? Some kind of –."

And then, it hit me. A hideous stench was rising from the jar. It was some kind of nasty fart cloud. Everyone else was starting to smell it and pinched their noses shut, waving their hands in front of their faces.

I punched Fevrile in the arm as hard as I could. "What kind of present is this?"

Fevrile, the dumb goof that he is, actually looked sad. "You don't like it?"

"Why would I like a jar filled with fart gas?" I yelled.

"But, I bought it special for you. That jar contains a fart from George Washington, one of the most famous humans who ever lived. I got it from a retired fart fairy at the swap meet."

I shoved the jar into Fevrile's hands. "Here, you keep it then. I get enough of the stinky stuff at work every day."

Fevrile's lower lip started to quiver. "But, you are always telling me how interested you are in history. I thought you'd like a historical fart for your birthday."

"I hate you, Fevrile! You ruined my birthday party!" I yelled as I stormed away and went to my room to sulk.

A few minutes later, my mom knocked on my door and walked into my room.

"Annabelle, I asked your friends to go home." She said, as she sat down on the bed next to me and rubbed my hair like I was a little puppy or something. "I'll leave you alone now, but we should talk about this tomorrow."

"Fine," I said.

My mom stood up. "Good. I'll let you know when dinner is ready," she said as she walked out of my room and shut the door.

Chapter Two: Mom is Worried

I WOKE UP THE NEXT DAY and took a shower. Fortunately, I did not have to go to work. I had taken the week off to celebrate my birthday.

After I got dressed, I went out to the kitchen to eat breakfast. My mom was there. She had prepared some delicious almond muffins with apricot jam and some lemongrass tea.

"Looks good," I said. "Thanks, mom."

My mom nodded and sat down as I started munching on a muffin. She looked at me very seriously. *Uh-oh*, I thought, *here it comes*.

"Annabelle, I am worried about how much you still dislike being a fart fairy. It's been almost five years, and I would think you would have gotten over it by now. I mean, you *saved the world* because you are a fart fairy."

I sighed. "Look, mom, I just…. I don't know. I want to be happy and like my job, but it is just so lame. Fevrile's present just reminded of that fact."

My mom took a deep breath and a sip of tea before responding. "Can't you just try to enjoy it? It seems like you have been making lots of new friends, and Jane, Cynthia and Sadie still like you. Isn't that enough?"

I shook my head. "I thought it would be, but I just can't get over the fact that I am a fart fairy. Even though I can request a job transfer after five more years, I just don't know how I can last that long."

"Look, Annabelle," said my mom, "if you are unhappy, the least you can do is stop making people around you suffer for that unhappiness. What you did to your brother yesterday was mean."

"He gives me a bottled fart for my birthday, but I'm the mean one?" I slammed my muffin down on the table, and it crumbled into little pieces. I was outraged. "Fevrile knows I don't like being a fart fairy. *He's* the one who is making *me* suffer."

"He did say it was because you liked history."

"Not the history of ancient farts! He could have just bought me a book or something." I pushed my plate and my mangled muffin away from me. "I'm not hungry anymore."

"Annabelle, I think you need to just calm down and accept your job. It was just a job the Queen gave you. *You* are not a fart fairy; it is just *your job*."

I shook my head. "Since when is something you have to do for at least ten years if not your entire life, *just* a job? That doesn't make any sense."

My mom sighed. "Why don't you get some hobbies or something, then? You can't change your job for the next five years, so find something else to do when you are not working."

"And that's another thing," I said, "why can't we change our jobs? Why can't we choose what we want to be?"

My mom looked at me with concern. "Annabelle, that is just how things are. It is how they have been for thousands of years. We can't change what makes us fairies. We just have to accept it."

"Mom, that just isn't right," I said. I got up and left.

Chapter Three: At the Sweet Drop

THAT EVENING, THE FORGOTTEN FAIRIES CLUB met at the Sweet Drop. It was Reggie, Bob, Rosalina and me. We were discussing Fevrile's gift.

"I can't believe he gave you an old fart! What is that brother of yours thinking?" said Rosalina.

I shrugged. "I don't think he thinks much. I mean, he *was* trying to get me something nice, but he is just so totally clueless sometimes."

"I don't know, I thought it was pretty cool," said Bob.

I looked at Bob and squinted my eyes. "What?" I said through clenched teeth.

"I mean, it's just that—" began Bob, trying to save himself from my wrath, when Reggie cut him off, saying, "Hey, who is that?"

We looked where Reggie was pointing and saw a fairy we had never seen before. She had disheveled auburn hair that looked like a rat's nest and which was clearly in need of a wash. Her dress wasn't much better, just a nondescript sack with stains and a few hastily-repaired rips in it, tied at the waist with some sort of rope.

The new fairy walked up to a table where several flower fairies were sitting. It looked like she was asking them if she could sit

down. They laughed at her and pointed at our table.

The new fairy started walking in our direction. When she got to our table, she said, "Hi, I'm Clara. The fairies at that other table said I should sit with you."

I looked over at the flower fairies who were laughing hysterically. I stuck my tongue out at them.

I wasn't exactly happy of the prospect of having a weird, filthy stranger sit with us, but I knew what it was like to be an outcast, so I said, "Sure. Grab a chair."

"Um, are you always so, well, dirty?" asked Rosalina.

Clara nodded. "Yep, comes with the job," she said as she waved the waiter over.

The waiter eyed her suspiciously. "Yes?"

"I'll take a cold glass of honeydew nectar, a fruit salad, and an acorn muffin," said Clara.

"I'm sorry, but you'll have to pay in advance," said the waiter.

"Hey," I said, my sense of justice offended. "You never charge us in advance."

"But, I know *you* can pay. I've never seen this one before."

Clara put her hand out to calm me down. "It's okay. This happens all the time when I visit fairy towns. I don't blame him." She plunged her hand in to a deep pocket in her sack dress and pulled out some shiny money grains. "Here you go," she said as she handed the money to the waiter.

"I'll be right back with your food," said the waiter after he counted the money.

"So, what kind of fairy are you that you get so dirty?" asked Bob.

"I am a primrose fairy," Clara said proudly.

"Aren't those wild roses?" I asked.

"Not exactly. The flower is rose-like, but the plant is a lot shorter. Doesn't matter though because they are the prettiest things in the world. Just like to grow in dusty terrain is all. I don't see many other fairies out there, so I just let myself go. I usually get pretty ripe by the time I take my annual vacation."

Now that she mentioned it, she was a bit stinky. Nothing like some of the farts I had to smell on a daily basis, but still not pleasant.

"I'm on a one-week vacation myself," I said. "It was my birthday yesterday."

"Well, happy birthday then," said Clara with enthusiasm. "You should stop by the Oak Tree Inn tomorrow, and I'll buy you dinner as a present."

I'm not sure I want to spend the day with a stinker like you, I thought. "Yeah, I guess we could do that," I said noncommittally.

The waiter arrived and set Clara's food down. She dug into the fruit salad with abandon, eating so quickly juice was running down her chin forming rivulets of mud as it drained through the dirt on her face.

"Oh, this is so good," she said.

At that moment, my friend Jane the rose fairy burst into the Sweet Drop. "Oh my gosh, a human almost grabbed me!" she screamed.

Everyone in the café rushed over to her. We all asked her if she was okay and what happened.

"I was taking a nap in a rose, just relaxing after a long day, when I looked up and saw a human woman walking by. I tucked myself into the flower petals, trying to hide, but the woman bent closer to the rose. She actually started pushing the petals aside and said, 'I see you in there.'" Jane paused to catch her breath.

"Did she really see you?" asked one of the flower fairies with a frightened voice.

"I don't know," said Jane. "Maybe. All I know is I was more scared than I had ever been. I pulled out a little pixie dust, sprinkled it on my wings, and flew out of the flower as fast as I could. I flew so fast, I don't think she even saw me fly by."

"Maybe she just thought you were a bug or something," said Reggie.

Jane looked at him angrily. "How dare you make such a ridiculous suggestion! She did not think I was a bug," she said as she smoothed her dress and primped her hair. "But, I do think she was a . . .a . . . fairy hunter."

Everyone gasped.

Even though Jane was well known for being a drama queen, this was different. If there were a fairy hunter around, we were all in danger. If the hunter was good, a fairy was bound to be caught eventually. A chill ran down my spine.

"I've had to deal with fairy hunters before," said Clara.

Jane looked at her. I could tell she had not noticed her until now. "Who or what are you?" asked Jane in a mean voice.

"Clara. Primrose fairy at your service," she said extending a hand.

Jane just looked at her hand. "I'm not touching that unless you wash it at least twice."

Clara just laughed. "You townsfolk afraid of a little dirt? Anyway, I had to deal with some fairy hunters about one hundred years ago. They were mean too. Wanted to kidnap a bunch of fairies for something they called a circus. I heard them say they were going to display the fairies and charge other humans to get a look at them."

We were all terrified listening to her story.

"What did you do?" asked Bob, sounding as scared as one of the black widows he had to wait on each day.

"We had to hide a lot. Eventually, they captured a couple lizard fairies. Lazy critters were sunning themselves on a rock. I never saw those fairies again, but the fairy hunters never came back."

Jane started to sway. "I think I'm going to faint," she said as she slowly fell to the floor. Slowly enough that Reggie could catch her.

"I got you," he said, leaping forward to catch her in his muscular arms.

Jane looked up at him and fluttered her eyelashes. "Oh, Reggie, you are so strong," she cooed.

Yuk, I thought, *where is a vomit fairy when you need one!*

"Anyway," continued Clara, "I think the best approach is just to be alert and hide or run away if you see any humans. That's why I didn't get caught and those lazy lizard fairies did."

Everyone was chattering as they began to go back to their tables. Jane left to sit with the flower fairies. Clara and the rest of us Forgotten Fairies went back to our table.

"Exciting stuff," said Clara, taking a sip of her nectar, a look of concern on her face. "I was looking for a little excitement in town, but nothing this dramatic."

Chapter Four: Oak Tree Inn

AT ABOUT FIVE O'CLOCK the next evening, I started getting ready for my birthday dinner with Clara. I wasn't sure exactly what sort of restaurant Clara had in mind, so I put on a nice outfit. It was fancy, but not too fancy, so I'd fit in just about anywhere she wanted to go.

I arrived at the Oak Tree Inn – which was, of course, carved into a large oak tree – just after 5:00 o'clock in the evening. The fairy at the front desk called up to Clara's room to tell her I had arrived.

"She says you can go up. Room fifteen," said the front-desk fairy.

I nodded. "Say, how did you get your job?" I asked, thinking I might want a similar job when my first ten years as a fart fairy were up and I could request a transfer.

He sighed. "I used to be a dog fairy, but one day, I got distracted and a dog picked me up in its mouth along with a tennis ball," he said. "I broke ten bones and dislocated a wing. I've never been the same."

"That is awful," I said, putting my hand over my mouth.

"When I recovered, the doctor ordered me to do only light-duty work, so the Fairy County job placement agency found me this."

"Do you miss being a dog fairy?"

He nodded sadly. "Everyday. This job is nice and quiet, but it is also dull and lonely and I never see any animals. And worst of all, I have to stay inside all day."

"Sorry about that," I said. "Um, so how do I get to Room Fifteen?"

He pointed towards some stairs. "Up those stairs to the second floor. Turn right. Second door on your left."

"Thank you," I said as I walked away.

The interior of the oak tree had been carved smooth by the carpenter fairies, whose work rivals or exceeds that of any human carpenter. Not only is the entire hotel exquisitely beautiful, but the carpenters carve away only the older wood in the center of the tree, not disturbing the living wood on the outer portions of the tree's trunk.

When I arrived at Clara's door, I knocked.

"Come in. It's open," said a voice through the door.

I opened the door and walked in. I saw a fairy I had never seen before. She was quite beautiful and dressed in a stunning pink and red dress, with a small sunflower pinned in her hair.

"Are you staying with Clara," I said, surprised that Clara had not mentioned her before.

The fairy started laughing so hard, I thought she would cry.

"What's so funny?" I said.

"Annabelle," she said in between laughs, "it's me. Clara."

I was almost speechless. "But . . . you . . . I mean, you were so dirty before and now . . . ."

"Yes, ma'am," Clara said. "It is amazing what a bath and a nice dress can do for a gal."

I stood there nodding. Clara might be the most beautiful fairy I had ever seen. I was amazed and a little jealous.

"There," said Clara, looking in the mirror and patting her hair with her hands, "all done." She turned to me. "What's there to do for fun in this town?"

I shrugged. "Not a lot. Usually we hang out at the Sweet Drop, but there are a couple of restaurants we could try."

Clara rolled her eyes. "Isn't there somewhere we can go dancing? I love dancing."

"Well, there is the Twisted Branch, but I've never been there. I heard it gets a bit weird sometimes," I said.

Clara clapped her hands together twice quickly. "Oh, goody. That sounds great. Let's get some nectar and food at the Sweet Drop and then go dancing."

I was a bit nervous. I had heard that some of the fairies that hung out at the Twisted Branch were troublemakers. My mom had told me I should wait until I was older to go there, but anyone over 500 was allowed to go.

"Well, okay, let's do it," I said.

Chapter Five: The Note

WHEN WE WALKED INTO THE SWEET DROP about ten minutes later, all conversation stopped and everyone stared at us. Well, actually, they were staring at Clara.

Jane, who was sitting with some other flower fairies, raised her hand and waved at us. "Annabelle, come over here. Bring your friend."

I looked at Clara, who winked at me and nodded. So, we walked over to the table.

Jane and all the other flower fairies were smiling widely. "So, aren't you going to introduce us to your friend?"

"Don't you remember her?" I said, rolling my eyes. It was obvious they just wanted to be friends with the pretty girl.

Jane looked more closely at Clara. She looked confused and shook her head.

"It's me, silly," said Clara in a sing-song voice. "The primrose fairy."

Jane and the other flower fairies let out a collective gasp. "But," stammered Jane, "you were so dirty and gross before. And now, you are so . . . beautiful."

I was glad Jane had been shocked about this. Even though we were friends, it still bothered me that she had distanced herself from me when she first learned I was a fart fairy. If I hadn't saved the world from that asteroid a few years ago, I'm pretty sure Jane would never have spoken to me again.

"I clean up well," said Clara.

"I guess so," said Jane. "Why don't you two sit down? We just ordered some apricot turnovers."

Clara smiled. "Oh, we would love to, but Annabelle's other friends are expecting us at their table."

Jane looked extremely disappointed. *Serves you right*, I thought.

"But, I will be in town for a few more days," said Clara. "Maybe we can sit with you tomorrow?"

Jane nodded. "That sounds lovely. Are you planning on making any more dramatic transformations?"

"Well, I was thinking about growing another head," said Clara as if she meant it.

We walked away from the flower fairies' table leaving them sad and perplexed. It looked like Jane was considering what she would do if Clara really did arrive tomorrow with two heads.

Reggie, Bob and Rosalina were at our usual table. When we got close to the table, Reggie and Bob both stood up.

"Here, Clara, take my chair," said Bob.

"No, Clara, take my chair. I insist," said Reggie.

Clara laughed. "Keep your chairs. I'll grab an empty one from the next table."

"What, no one offers me a chair?" I said, also grabbing an empty chair from a nearby table.

Reggie and Bob stared at Clara as she grabbed her chair and sat down. They kept staring at her like no one else was in the room. I noticed a few of the other boys in the Sweet Drop were doing the same thing.

"Really?" I said, looking at Rosalina. She smirked and shrugged her shoulders.

Clara looked at me and laughed. "I see this sort of behavior with humans all the time. They walk by the primrose plant all year without noticing it, like it is just some ugly shrub. But, when it blooms, they suddenly notice it and comment to each other about how pretty it is."

"So, you knew this was going to happen?" I said.

"It always does. I come in to town and most people ignore me. Then, I get cleaned up and everyone notices me."

"You must like the attention," I said, feeling a bit sorry for myself that I couldn't get this sort of attention.

"When no one notices you all year, it is nice to get some attention once in a while. It lets you know you are still alive." Clara paused, lost in thought. "But, most of the time I prefer being anonymous."

"Let's order some food," said Rosalina, waving her arm to get the attention of the waiter.

After eating, we all ordered warm, spiced nectar for dessert. Clara and I had been there nearly an hour, and most of the other fairies had stopped staring at her.

Clara took a last sip of her nectar and put her mug down on the table. "So, Annabelle, are you ready to go dancing?"

"Dancing?" said Bob and Reggie simultaneously.

I nodded. "We are going to the Twisted Branch."

"Do you all want to come too?" asked Clara.

"I think I'll pass," said Rosalina. "I don't have the week off like Annabelle, so I need to get to sleep. It's cold season among the humans, and the snot is everywhere."

Bob suddenly looked sad. "I want to go, but several of the black widows are going through some really tough times. Some humans squished their egg sacks. I'll need to be there for them first thing in the morning, so I need a good night's sleep too."

"Well, fleas basically take care of themselves, so I'll come with you," said Reggie.

"Great," said Clara, "let's go."

As we walked out the exit of the Sweet Drop, we noticed little white flakes falling from the sky.

"Snow?" said Clara.

"It can't be snow," I said. "It never snows here. Besides, it isn't very cold."

I picked up one of the flakes from the ground. It was actually a small piece of paper. When I flipped it over, I saw there were words written on it. It said:

> *Fairies. I mean you no harm. I am a fairyologist. I wish only to learn more about you and your ways. Please come to my house at*

> *785 Main Street and speak with me.*
> *Sincerely, Mia.*

I felt a cold chill run down my spine as I read those words. A human knew exactly where we lived.

"What do you think this means?" I said, handing the paper to Clara.

Clara read the note and scrunched her eyebrows. "I am not sure, but I know we aren't going dancing tonight."

"What should we do?" said Reggie.

"Why don't you and Annabelle alert everyone in the Sweet Drop and then go home. I'll fly over to the Queen's palace and make sure she knows about this," said Clara. "We could be dealing with a very clever fairy hunter."

Chapter Six: Be Careful

BY THE NEXT MORNING, every fairy knew about the mysterious notes that had fallen from the sky. If they had not found a note themselves, they had heard about them from a friend.

The Queen deemed the situation serious enough to make an announcement on the County's FAME (the *Fairy Automatic Message Enunciator*) to ensure that all fairies were aware of the possible danger. She said:

> *Fairies. As you probably know, a human named Mia, claiming to be a fairyologist, has blanketed our Fairy County with notes. Mia claims to only want to learn about us. But, do not be fooled.*

While we know there are some good humans, the history of fairy-human interaction is filled with tragedy and exploitation. Humans seem unable to separate their curiosity from their greed. In the end, fairies always get hurt.

Do not speak with Mia. Do not go near her house unless on official fairy business. Fairy security depends on not being seen by humans.

Thank you for your attention. If you see or hear anything else about this Mia, I order you to come to the palace and inform me immediately.

I had been eating breakfast with my family when I heard the announcement.

"Hmmmm," my dad mumbled as the FAME turned off.

"What is it, dear?" said my mom as she took a sip of chicory tea.

"Why would a human go through the trouble of making hundreds of little notes for fairies to read if she only wanted to do bad things to us?"

"I don't know," my mom said, "but I do know that some humans can be very devious. This is probably just a trick to get us fairies to believe she is different from all the other fairy hunters."

My dad slowly rubbed his chin with his hand and then said, "You could be right, but it seems like most of the evil humans I've heard about just try to trap fairies like animals without going through the trouble of writing to us."

"Yeah," said Fevrile, "maybe it would be a good thing for a fairy to try and talk to her. Maybe she is not so bad."

"Well," said my mom, "I don't care what you and your father *think,* I don't want anyone

in this family going near that person. She knows we exist and will be looking for us." I could tell Mom was getting angry and a little scared.

"Jane said a human tried to grab her a couple days ago," I said, hoping to freak my mom out a little more.

"What! Why didn't you tell us before?" my mom said. She was on the verge of hysteria now.

"Yep," I said in between bites of porridge. "I wasn't sure I believed her. She loves attention. But, now I suppose maybe it really happened."

"Children," said my dad, "listen carefully. While I have more faith in humans than your mother does, I do not want either of you being captured by one. Since both of you have to do your fairy work near humans, I want you to be extra vigilant."

Fevrile and I nodded.

"Gosh, Annabelle, you are lucky you have a few more days off work," said Fevrile. "Maybe this will all be over with by then."

"Maybe," I said.

As we sat in silence, eating the rest of our breakfast, I thought back to the Queen's words. Something did not make sense.

I looked at my parents. "Mom, Dad, what did the Queen mean by 'tragedy and exploitation' of fairies by humans? I've heard of humans trying to put fairies on display in circuses. Is that it?"

My parents looked at each other. I could tell this was something very serious.

"Go ahead and tell them," said my mom with a sigh.

"Annabelle. Fevrile. You know how you learned fairy history in school?"

We both nodded.

"You only learn the history that is necessary for you to understand why fairies are important to the balance of nature and about the fairies who helped shape our modern society. They leave out the darker parts of the past."

My dad was starting to creep me out. I looked over at Fevrile. His usual goofy grin had been replaced with an expression of concern.

"They also give you only the basics of human history, because humans are normally of little concern to fairies except when they upset the balance of nature, which is something they tend to do. But there is one more thing some humans do."

My dad paused. He reached over and took my mom's hand. They looked at each other and she nodded for him to continue.

"There are humans called witches and wizards. Humans believe they are magical and evil. It is true, they are evil because their magic comes from . . . an enslaved fairy."

"No," whispered Fevrile.

"Yes," my dad continued. "They trap fairies and, through some means not entirely understood by fairy science, force the fairies to use their magical abilities on behalf of the human."

"That is terrible!" I said. "Why do we bother helping humans at all if they would do such things?"

"Now, now, Annabelle," said my mom, "most humans are perfectly fine and have no bad intentions toward fairies. After all, fairies go wrong too sometimes and have to spend some time in fairy prison."

I blushed. In a fit of anger, I had used my magic to make a little girl poop her pants, and I spent a month in prison because of it. "But, Mom, there is a difference between making a dumb mistake and being evil," I said.

"Yes, the important thing is learning a lesson from your mistake."

"Dad?" said Fevrile. "If a witch or wizard captures a fairy, do they ever escape?"

"I've never heard of any of them escaping on their own, but most of them are rescued.

Once the fairy world learns of a captured fairy, it stops at nothing to free the fairy."

Chapter Seven: Mia's House

I HAD PLANS TO MEET CLARA after breakfast. We were going to spend the day shopping at the fairy market and visiting some of my friends. Clara wanted to see what sort of fairy work they did.

As I flew toward the Oak Tree Inn, I felt a telltale tingle in my toes alerting me that a human needed to fart. Even though I was on vacation, I thought I'd head over to the location of the tingle and say hello to my old teacher, Laverne, who was working the morning shift.

As I got closer to the location of the tingle, I heard Laverne's gravelly voice calling to me from behind a tree.

"Annabelle! Annabelle! Get over here now!" she said with urgency.

I looked around and saw her waving at me. I flew toward her.

"What are you doing here?" she said.

"I felt the tingle and thought I'd come talk to you for a few minutes."

Laverne nodded and then pointed toward a house. "The tingle is coming from that house down there."

"Duh," I said, rolling my eyes. "I've been a fart fairy for five years. I can figure out where a tingle is coming from."

"But, look at the address," she said, clearly frightened.

I looked down and saw the numbers on the house: 785. I looked for a street sign and read "Main Street."

"Oh my gosh, Laverne, it is the address in the notes!"

She nodded. "Yes. Keep your distance. I am going to shazaam the fart from here."

After Laverne did a shazaam, we both felt the tingle go away.

"Laverne, if this human really is a fairyologist, do you think she knows about fart fairies?"

"I don't know and I don't care."

"But, don't you think it would be interesting to try and talk to her?" I said.

"Don't you remember what happened the last time you started snooping around the room of a fairy-obsessed human?"

How could I forget? I thought. *That little girl captured me in a jar and I ended up in prison.*

"Annabelle, just forget about it. Stay away from that house."

I nodded.

"Oh, another tingle. Feels like a big one," said Laverne, "I have to go. See you later."

I waved to Laverne as she flew away. I sat in the tree staring at the house, wondering what was happening inside of it.

After a few minutes, I was about to leave and meet Clara when the door of the house opened. A young woman walked out of the door.

She was wearing jeans and a white t-shirt. She did not look evil. She walked to her car, got in, and drove away.

The house was empty!

I quickly flew down to the house and landed on a windowsill that was partly hidden behind a bush. I peeked in the window.

I had never seen so many things about fairies outside of a fairy school classroom. And it wasn't the usual pink fairy dolls or flower fairy posters that most humans have. There were life-like paintings and statues. It looked like hundreds of books about fairies. There were even antique tapestries depicting scenes of fairy gatherings.

I flew around the house to another window. I saw a desk, covered with papers and books. There were charts on the wall and a large map of the area with various locations circled or marked with pushpins.

There were photographs of flowers and trees. One of the trees looked a lot like where the Oak Tree Inn was located.

"She's studying us," I said quietly. "She really is a fairyologist."

I rushed away from the house. I was so excited. I couldn't wait to tell Clara.

Chapter Eight: The Conversation

I FLEW TO THE OAK TREE INN. Clara was waiting in the lobby, looking slightly annoyed because I was about fifteen minutes late.

I waved, "Clara. Hi, sorry I'm late. I have a really good reason."

Clara shrugged her shoulders. "It's okay. Let's just go eat."

I grabbed her by the shoulders and looked at her. "No, really, it's a great reason!" Then I looked around suspiciously. "Do you think we could eat breakfast in your room?" I asked.

"Uh, I guess so," Clara said uncertainly.

"Good. I've got a secret."

We ordered breakfast from the front desk and asked it to be delivered to the room, then we went up the stairs. I had to encourage Clara to walk faster. I really wanted to tell her, but did not want anyone else to hear.

"This better be a good secret," said Clara. "I'm starving."

"Don't worry," I said as I watched Clara open the door to her room. "It is."

We walked into the room and Clara sat down on a chair with a sigh. "Okay, what's this great secret?" she asked.

I walked over to the door and locked it. Clara raised a curious eyebrow. "I don't want anyone walking in unannounced."

Clara leaned forward to listen. "What could you tell me that requires a locked door?"

I took a deep breath and said, "I saw the fairyologist. She looks nice. I went inside her house."

"You what?!" screamed Clara. "That is the stupidest thing I've ever heard. I should—."

Just then, there was a knock on the door. A muffled voice from the other side of the door said, "Your breakfast is here, ladies."

An older fairy, dressed in a tuxedo, pushed a cart in with a silver dome on top of it. He lifted the dome to reveal acorn muffins, blueberries, strawberries and some beans (for me, of course).

Clara leapt up to the cart and grabbed a pile of food and started stuffing it in her face. I picked up an acorn muffin and nibbled it.

The older fairy just stood there, waiting for something. Clara looked at me. "You need to tip him. You are the one who wanted to get room service, so you tip him."

I hadn't stayed in a hotel by myself before, but I had seen my dad tip waiters. "Uh, what's a good tip?"

"Two money grains," said the waiter.

"Two grains?!" I couldn't believe it. I could have bought a day's worth of food for that amount. "That's ridiculous."

"Pay him," said Clara as acorn crumbs sprayed from her mouth.

"Here," I said, slapping two grains into the man's hands. "Don't spend it all in one place."

He smiled. "How could I? That is a lot of money." Then he winked at me and left.

"Oh, you . . . . Oh!" I said as I slammed the door and locked it again.

Clara was laughing at me with her mouth full, and blueberry juice was dripping on her chin.

"Oh, be quiet." I said, as the anger passed.

When Clara calmed down a bit, I described what I had seen at the fairyologist's house, and then asked, "So, what do you think? Do you want to go talk to the fairyologist with me this afternoon?"

Clara leveled her gaze at me, though it was a little difficult to take her seriously with the juice and crumbs on her mouth. "What are you talking about? Don't you remember what the Fairy Queen said?"

"I know, but she looked nice. I think she really just wants to learn more about fairies."

Clara shook her head. "So, you want humans to know more about fairies? So more of them will come trying to find us? That's why fairies have survived this long, we keep to ourselves so no humans believe in us except children. And adults never believe children when they tell them they just saw a fairy."

I sighed. "Don't you ever want to do something other than what you know you *should* do? Wouldn't you like to speak with a human who studies fairies and see what she thinks about us? What she knows about us?"

Clara took a drink of her nectar and swallowed hard. "Maybe that would be interesting, but the only human-fairy interaction I've ever seen was those horrible men kidnapping those two lizard fairies."

"Oh, come on, you don't think that will happen to me, do you?"

Clara nodded. "Yes, I do. You cannot trust humans."

"But . . . ," I tried to continue, but Clara put her hand up indicating that I should stop.

"We are done talking about this, Annabelle. I should report you to the Queen, but since you are my friend, I won't. But if you bring the topic up again, I will tell the Queen everything you just said."

"Fine," I said, completely dejected. I had really hoped that Clara would agree to go talk with Mia, but I guess she wasn't as adventurous as I had hoped.

"Eat something," said Clara.

I picked at the food, but did not enjoy it at all. I was depressed. The chance to speak with an adult human and help her understand fairies was so exciting, but now I would have to just spend my life wondering what she might have said to me.

After we finished eating, we went shopping at the fairy market. Normally, I would have enjoyed it, but this time I just followed behind Clara like an obedient dog. Clara loved shopping, since she only got to town once per year. Everything seemed new to her, and it was exciting and different.

About an hour later, we met Reggie, Bob and Rosalina at the Sweet Drop. Everyone was having a good time, except me. Reggie and Bob were hanging on Clara's every word and saying how much they liked the clothes and knickknacks she had purchased at the market.

I kept thinking about Mia, and what we might talk about. I wanted to ask Reggie, Bob and Rosalina if they wanted to talk to Mia, but I knew Clara would follow through on her threat to tell the Queen, so I kept quiet and moped.

"What's wrong, Annabelle?" asked Reggie, finally noticing I was in a bad mood.

I shrugged my shoulders. "Just not in a talking mood today, I guess."

"So, what do you guys think about the fairy hunter?" asked Rosalina.

"I don't like her," snapped Clara, shooting a quick glance at me, warning me not to say something I shouldn't.

"Well," said Bob, "on the one hand, I think it is pretty freaky, but on the other hand, it seems kind of cool, too."

"Cool? How?" asked Clara.

Bob shrugged. "You know, something different and exciting. Something to think about and pass the time. Even the black widows I was tending to yesterday had heard about it. Of course, they are so paranoid, they think it is all a plot to capture the black widow fairies so this Mia person can steal their precious egg sacks. Oh! Those spiders annoy me so much!"

"Calm down, Bob," said Rosalina, putting a hand on his shoulder. "I don't like this fairy hunter business at all. After Jane almost got snatched, I think the Queen is right to keep us away from her."

I frowned and then looked at Reggie. "What do you think?"

"I guess," he began, "that I would very much like to know what Mia wants and why. I don't really want human adults knowing too much about fairies because some might misuse the information. On the other hand, maybe the knowledge we could gain from Mia would open up new possibilities for advancement in fairy society and culture."

We were all staring at Reggie. None of us expected such a thoughtful response from such a bulky guy. We had all just assumed he wasn't that smart.

"What do you mean, new avenues for fairy culture?" asked Clara.

"Remember in history class? It seemed like every time the fairies encountered some very different situation or group they had to deal with, they grew as a society. When the meteor hit the earth, the fairies had to learn to work together very closely. When the bodily function and insect fairies finally gained the respect of the flower fairies, society changed for the better and became more inclusive. Maybe this is what the fairies need right now, ideas from the outside."

"Ideas?! You think Mia will bring ideas?!" yelled Clara. "She will only bring destruction and ruin! She will destroy us!"

I hadn't seen anyone flip out like that since my dad caught me trying to put Fevrile in the washing machine when we were little kids. Everyone in the Sweet Drop was staring at Clara. It was dead silent.

Clara looked around. Realizing what a scene she had made, she apologized and sat down.

"I don't get it, Clara," I said. "You know that people had the wrong idea about you when you first came into town all dirty and stinky. But, now that they know you, they like you. Our impression of Mia is based on stories and past history, not who she is."

"Rules exist for a reason, Annabelle, because they are almost always right. I don't want to break a rule and have the consequences be exactly what I expect."

I sighed. There was no reasoning with her. I would have to do this on my own.

Chapter Nine: Annabelle Does It

THE NEXT DAY I WOKE UP and decided that this was the day. I only had two more days of vacation, and I needed to make contact now. If Mia turned out to be a kind fairyologist, I would want to speak with her in more detail, and I needed the extra day.

I told my mom I was going to see Clara again, but instead I flew straight to Mia's house. Her car was in the driveway, so I assumed she was home. I cautiously approached one of the windows and looked in. She was there, sitting at a table looking at a book.

I studied her.

I had to be right about this or else the consequences could be disastrous, but there was nothing to indicate she was actually an evil fairy hunter in disguise. She seemed to just be reading and thinking. I suspect someone evil would be cackling and rubbing her hands together, so there were no obvious signs of evil.

I decided to risk it. *Why not?* The worst that happens is I get captured, but the best that happens is I open up a whole new line of communication between fairies and humans.

I flew away from the window looking for some way to get into the house. After checking three windows, I noticed that one of them was cracked open a few inches. I walked into the house.

I fluttered through the house, trying to find my way to the room in which Mia was sitting. It was difficult because I had never tried to find my way through a human house before. So many rooms and passages!

As I flew slowly through the house, I heard some rustling coming from the room just in front of me. It must be Mia turning the pages of her book. I landed on the floor and crept to the doorway. I peaked in. There she was.

This is it, I thought. My heart started pounding and my stomach felt upset, much like during the Great Selecting ceremony when I unleashed my unfortunate fart on the Queen. But, I hadn't been eating any burritos lately, so this time it was just nerves.

The direct approach is best, so I put my nervousness aside and flew right up to Mia and landed on the book in front of her.

"Hi, I'm Annabelle," I said.

Mia's eyes got as wide as the moon, she screamed and then quickly pushed her chair back and stood up. I thought she might think I was a bug, so I ducked behind a large paperweight on her desk.

"Oh my gosh, a real . . . a real . . . ." Then she stopped, and clutched her hand to her chest. She started fanning herself with her hand and looked at me. "You are a fairy, aren't you?"

I came out from my hiding place. "Yes, I got your note."

Mia's eyes were welling up with tears. "Finally, after all these years, I get to speak to a real fairy," she said in a soft voice. "My parents thought I was crazy, but I knew fairies existed."

"We sure do," I said. "We just like to keep it a secret." I looked her up and down. "You aren't a fairy hunter, are you?"

Mia looked highly offended. "A fairy hunter? Of course not. I've . . . well, let's say I've heard about those evil people, and I would never, ever enslave another creature."

I believed her. Now we could get down to business.

"So," I began, "why do you want to talk to a fairy?"

Mia plopped down in her chair. I could tell she was still in a daze from meeting a real fairy. "Well, I saw a fairy once when I was a little girl, and I never forgot it. I told everyone about it, but no one ever believed me. I have dedicated my life to studying fairies in the hope that I would be able to meet one and prove they exist."

"You aren't going to put me in a circus, are you?"

Mia laughed. It was a kind laugh. "No. I just want to write a book about fairies and their habits. I don't think people appreciate how important fairies are."

"No, they don't," I said.

Mia continued. "I mean, if it weren't for fairies, the entire world would fall apart. It took me a while to figure this out. At first, I thought fairies were just a magical race of mischievous creatures who existed to have fun, but as I studied more and more, I came to the conclusion that without fairies, nature could not continue." She paused and looked at me hopefully. "Am I right?"

I have to admit I was amazed that she had figured all of that out. "Um, yeah, actually you are."

Mia squealed like a little girl eating a pink cupcake on her birthday. "I'm so glad." She clapped her hands, and then looked at me and asked, "So what sort of fairy are you?"

I was dreading this moment. *Remember, Annabelle, the direct approach is best.* "Uh, I'm a fart fairy."

To my surprise, Mia did not laugh, but smiled and then nodded very seriously. "I knew it. If fairies are the reason nature works, there had to be fairies who were responsible for every aspect of nature."

"Yeah, unfortunately," I said glumly.

"You don't like being a fart fairy?"

I shook my head.

"But, I thought all fairies were happy," said Mia.

I laughed. "We are a lot like humans. We have similar emotions and desires. Believe it or not, I want to be a history teacher in our fairy schools."

"A history teacher, really? Why?"

"I used to think all non-flower fairies were lame, but I had no good reason for it. It was just prejudice. I thought back to school, and realized I never learned anything about fart fairies or scab fairies or snot fairies or any of that stuff. It was just wrong."

"So," said Mia, "you want to teach the history of all the fairies, even the ones no one talks about?"

I nodded. "The Forgotten Fairies is what I call them."

"That's . . . that's really thoughtful," said Mia. She paused in contemplation and then asked, "Would you like something to eat?"

"Sure, what do you have?"

After a nice snack (almonds and lemonade), we sat down and talked.

Mia asked me all sorts of questions, taking notes the entire time. She responded with a series of "oohs" and "ahhs" and the occasional, "I knew it" or "I don't believe it."

The best part was when I told her about the asteroid.

"Asteroid, what do you mean?"

"You know, five years ago. The asteroid that almost destroyed life on earth," I said.

She shook her head. "I don't know anything about an asteroid. There was nothing on the news about it."

"So, no humans know about it?" I asked incredulously.

"I don't know," she said. "Maybe some people in the government knew about it but didn't tell us. If the asteroid was so big that it could destroy the earth, I am sure someone saw it."

"That's just great. We fairies save the world and no one knows but the fairies." I was angry.

Mia looked at me quizzically. "But, isn't that how fairies want it. To operate in the shadows?"

It sounded so sinister when she said it that way, but she was right. We keep to ourselves and don't want anyone else to know what we do.

"Yes, and that is why I came to talk to you. Our Queen said not to, but I think this is best to open lines of communication between humans and fairies."

Mia's eyes got wide. "You disobeyed your Queen to be here?"

I nodded. "I'm not proud of it, but you seemed like a nice person and I wanted to help you out."

"I'm honored, but won't you be in serious trouble?"

"Only if they find out. You won't tell them, will you?"

Mia laughed. "I can't even find them. How could I tell them?"

I laughed too.

And then, I heard a loud smashing sound, heavy footsteps, and saw two human men wearing masks and dressed in black running into the room. As I jumped into the air to fly away, I heard Mia scream, "No!" I looked back to see the men spraying some sort of gas into the room.

Mia collapsed in a heap. I flew as fast as I could, but the gas cloud caught up with me. Suddenly, I couldn't feel my wings and fell to the ground.

As I lay there on the ground, struggling to stay conscious, I saw one of the masked men reaching toward me. As his gloved hand closed around my body, I passed out.

Chapter Ten: Captured

WHEN I REGAINED CONSCIOUSNESS, I was inside a brightly-lit room. Almost everything I could see was painted white or was made of shiny metal.

As I stood up to get a better look, I was overwhelmed with dizziness and quickly sat down again.

"Annabelle, Annabelle."

It was Mia's voice, but where was she. I started frantically looking around for her.

"Annabelle, over here. Over here," I heard her shout.

I swiveled my head back and forth until I finally saw her. She was inside a metal cage about twenty feet away. She was waving at me, but her hands were in handcuffs!

"Where are we?" I said, hoping it was loud enough for her to hear me.

"A government laboratory."

"What? Why?"

"Those men at my house work for the government. I think they were spying on me, and I led them to you. I'm sorry." Mia started crying.

"It's not your fault. If I had listened to the Queen, we wouldn't be here," I said as I started crying too. "What do they want with us?"

Mia wiped the tears from her eyes. "I think they want to figure out a way to . . . to . . . harness fairy magic."

I was horrified. "What do you mean 'harness' the magic?"

"I can answer that question," said a man with a deep growling voice.

I looked over and saw a man who had just entered the room. He was wearing a lab coat and holding a clipboard.

He continued, "We knew about the rumors that witches and wizards actually used captured fairies, so we wanted to capture a fairy of our own to see what kinds of weapons we can make using fairy magic."

This was crazy. I thought. *Time to get out of here.*

"Try harnessing this, you meany," I yelled as I summoned my most powerful "Shazaam" ever. I was going to make him fart himself silly while we escaped.

"SHAZAAM!" I screamed.

But, nothing happened. The man smiled at me.

"What the heck?" I said, completely stupefied by the ineffectiveness of my magic.

"Other fairies have tried that before. We developed a magic shield to prevent that."

Wow, humans are really clever. "Wait, what do you mean, other fairies?"

"We've captured a few before, but were never very successful in harnessing their magic. The experiments always ended in . . . um . . . failure."

"You are evil!" I yelled at the man.

"That will be for history to judge, not you."

"Whose history?" I asked.

The man snickered. "The best part is that Mia led us right to you. I knew that she would. That's why we fired her."

I looked over at Mia in shock. "You used to work here experimenting on fairies?"

Mia was crying. "I never experimented on fairies. I thought the government just wanted to learn about fairies, so when they recruited me out of college, I was honored. I could actually make a living pursuing my life's passion. But, after a couple years, I realized they wanted my knowledge for evil. I tried to get them to change, but they fired me instead."

"Yes," said the man in his low, sinister voice, "and we knew you'd keep looking for fairies and eventually would contact one. It is so much easier to capture fairies when they are out in the open."

I put my hands on my knees and started rocking back and forth. "Why didn't I listen to the Queen? Why didn't I listen to my mom? Why didn't I listen to Clara?"

"Because you have an adventurous soul, Annabelle," said the man. "We were listening in on your conversation with Mia. And, just so you know, we knew about the asteroid. We thought it was the end of the world, but we watched through telescopes while you fairies saved us. I'm honored to be in the presence of the person who came up with the idea."

"Then let me go," I screamed.

"Sorry, but I can't let an opportunity like this slip through my fingers," he said. "I'll let you get some rest to regain your strength. We want you in top shape when we begin the experiments tomorrow morning."

Chapter Eleven: The Experiments

THE LABORATORY WAS COLD, and I shivered all night. I slept a little, but was awake most of the time, worrying and trying to stay warm.

I noticed a sliver of moonlight coming through a narrow window on the opposite side of the room. I remembered when I had been high above the earth, directing Operation Blast Shield to deflect the asteroid. I had noticed the moon then. It seemed so huge and bright. Now, it seemed as dim and distant as a flashlight on the other side of a wide valley.

When I did manage to sleep, I had horrible dreams. I was falling down a bottomless pit and my wings were broken. I could do nothing but fall and fall, not knowing when, or even *if*, I would ever hit the bottom.

A clicking sound woke me up. It was my teeth chattering. I was freezing. I sat up and pulled my knees to my chest to try and warm up.

I started thinking about what these horrible humans were going to do to me. I kept thinking back to my dad's story about the wizards and witches who enslaved fairies. I assumed that would be my fate.

I started crying. I'd never get to see my family and friends again.

I looked over at Mia. She was awake, staring at me. I could tell from her eyes that she had been crying earlier during the night.

When our eyes met, I asked between sobs, "How could you?"

"I swear, I didn't know this would happen," she said.

"But you knew they were experimenting on fairies."

"No, I never knew they had actually captured a fairy. I'd never even seen a fairy until I met you, Annabelle," Mia said, and then sighed heavily. "I told them that if they did catch a fairy, we should learn from it, not experiment on it. Anyway, what was I supposed to do after they fired me?"

I stood up and pointed my finger at her. "You should have told someone else. Doesn't your human government have someone in charge who could have stopped this?"

"Yes, but almost no adults believe in fairies. They would have just thought I was crazy. They would have added that to the list of reasons they fired me."

I was yelling now, "You should have made them believe! It would have kept me out of this mess."

"Annabelle, I – "

"I wish I'd never met you, Mia," I said, turning my back to her.

Mia didn't say anything after that. She just sobbed quietly in her cage.

We stayed that way for about an hour. I saw the sliver of moonlight turn into a sliver of the sunrise. And then, the door opened and

the man walked in with another man in a white coat.

"Sleep well?" he asked in his deep voice.

"Like you care," I said.

He laughed and then looked at Mia. "We are moving you to another area. We don't want you interfering with our experiments."

Mia said nothing as the second man opened the door to her cage and grabbed her arm. As he led Mia away, I suddenly felt bad for what I said. I yelled, "No, let her stay. I don't want to be alone."

The man laughed. He was laughing so hard that he did not notice when Mia stepped on the foot of her escort, sending him to the ground, howling in pain. She quickly leapt at the laughing man, knocking him to the ground.

"Yeah, Mia!" I shouted.

Mia ran over to my cage and was fumbling with the lock to let me out.

"When I get you out of this cage, fly away as fast as you can and never come back," she said.

"Hurry," I said as I watched her trying to get the lock open.

If she had not been in handcuffs, she might have succeeded in freeing me. But, she was having trouble opening the lock, and that gave the two men enough time to recover from their surprise and jump up and grab her.

"No!" she screamed. "No!"

The man with the gravelly voice growled at Mia. "Fine. If you like your little friend here so much, we'll let you stay and watch. But don't say we didn't try to protect you from what you will see."

They tossed Mia in a chair and chained her to it with another set of handcuffs.

I looked at the man in horror. "What do you mean protect her from what she will see? What are you going to do to me?"

The man smiled. "Nothing much, at first. Just relax."

He was right. The experiments started simply.

The first thing they did was insert little clamps into my cage. They grabbed me with these clamps and started measuring my height, weight and wingspan.

Next, they wanted to test my eyesight and reaction time. I don't know why they bothered. I am a fairy, so my eyesight is perfect and my reaction time is so quick that only a few small insects can rival it.

I did not cooperate with the testing, but they had machines that could measure most of these things even if I did not cooperate.

After a couple hours, they started with the more cruel tests. They tested how fast I could fly by putting me in a tube and then putting a flame at one end so I had to fly away or else I would be burned.

"Stop this," pleaded Mia. "You are going to hurt her."

The man looked over at her. "We need to know all of her capabilities so we can determine the best weapons to make from her."

"Wait," said Mia with a look of shock on her face. "*From* her?"

"I meant from her magic," he said, looking like a liar.

"I hate you," I said to the man as he turned off the flame. He didn't respond.

I watched as he and the other man began to set up another experiment. They put together two large white boxes, but I could not see what was inside either of them. Then, they picked up a glass bottle filled with a clear liquid, and poured it in an opening at the top of one of the boxes.

"Be careful pouring that stuff," said the man. "Skin contact would be bad."

Oh my goodness, what are they going to do to me? I thought.

It took them a few more minutes to finish setting up the experiment.

The man with the deep, mean voice put on a pair of rubber gloves and started walking to my cage.

"Ok, fairy," he snarled. "Now the real fun begins."

I cowered in the corner of my cage as I watched him slowly unlock the door and reach his glove-covered hand in to grab me. And then . . . .

Chapter Twelve: Rescued

CRASH!

Everyone in the room turned just in time to see the small window, the one through which I'd watched the moon, shattering into a thousand tiny pieces.

Then, through the window came the most glorious sight I have ever seen: My dad, Fevrile, Clara, and fifty other fairies.

The man was dumbfounded. He forgot that my cage was still open. I took to the air, zooming from the cage as fast as I could to my dad, Fevrile and Clara.

"How did you find me?" I asked, hugging them as tears rolled down my cheeks.

Clara laughed. "I knew you wouldn't stay away from Mia, so I followed you. I saw you go into her house. I was waiting outside to confront you, when they caught you. I convinced a nearby crow to let me ride on her so I could follow you."

Fevrile was too excited not to interrupt. "Yeah, Clara followed you and then reported everything to the Queen and we put together this rescue mission and I insisted on coming in case I needed to give anyone a fever and I just . . . . Wow! I am so glad you are alive."

As I hugged Fevrile and my dad, my dad asked, "Did they hurt you?"

I shook my head. "No, not really."

In a well-coordinated attack, the other fairies unleashed their powers on the two men. The men started barfing and coughing

and sneezing all at the same time. Then, when they were on the floor twitching in a pile of goo, a couple of ice fairies unleashed and froze them into position, leaving their heads unfrozen so they could breathe.

I flew down to the man with the deep voice and asked, "Do you understand the power of fairy magic now, you meany?"

"Please don't kill me," he begged.

My dad was now standing by my side. "Fairies don't kill things. We help things live. We maintain the balance of nature."

"Then, what are you going to do?" asked the man.

"Oh, you'll see," said my dad with a sneer. I was a little scared, actually.

That is when I noticed five strangely-dressed fairies flying, or maybe I should call it floating, across the room toward the two men encased in frozen vomit. The fairies were wearing thick, ornate robes, covered with ancient patterns.

"Who are they?" I asked my dad as quietly as I could.

"Memory erasing fairies."

"What?" said the man, terrified.

My dad looked down at the man with contempt and said, "I told you we fairies maintain the balance of nature. When a human gains too much knowledge of fairies or proof that fairies exist, we have to erase their memories so they cannot use that knowledge to unbalance nature."

Both men now looked genuinely terrified as they watched the memory erasing fairies approach.

"How come I've never heard about these fairies?" I asked.

My dad smiled. "No one knows about them except a few fairies in the top levels of government. I only know about them because I was involved in an incident shortly before you were born in which we had to rescue a fairy from a witch and erase her memory."

I nodded. And then, *oh no,* I thought. I looked over at Mia. "Does that mean you have to erase her memory too?"

My dad nodded gravely.

"But, she tried to save me. She . . . she's my friend," I said.

"I know, Annabelle, but it cannot be helped. There can be no exceptions. If you want to talk to her for a few minutes before we do it, you may."

I flew over to Mia, who had tears running down her face.

"I'm sorry, Annabelle. I wish none of this had happened."

"Me too," I said as I used my wand to zap the lock on her handcuffs and free her. She touched my wing with her finger.

"I've waited my entire life to meet a fairy, and now I will never remember it. I feel so sad, but I am happy that I did get to know you. Maybe you will remember me as a good human."

"I will, I will," I said as I started to cry.

"Annabelle," said my dad, "it is time."

"Dad, can't she keep even one memory of our friendship?" I begged.

"The Queen's Counsel discussed that prior to sending the rescue mission. It was agreed that if Mia was a good human, we could leave her with the memory that fairies are real, but with no specific facts to support that memory."

Mia looked at my dad and smiled. "Oh, thank you, sir."

"Thanks, Dad," I said as I hugged him tight.

"And, Mia," my dad continued, "we've already removed all evidence of your meeting with Annabelle from the files in your house."

Mia nodded and then looked at the mysterious memory erasing fairies. "Will it hurt?" she asked my dad.

"No."

Chapter Thirteen: Homecoming

ONCE THE MEMORY ERASING FAIRIES were done with their work, the sleep fairies put the two men and Mia in to a deep sleep. The other fairies cleaned up any evidence that we were ever there, destroyed all evidence of fairy existence, and then we left.

Outside there were several crows waiting to fly us back home. The journey only took about thirty minutes, meaning that the government laboratory was not very far from our town.

When we got home, my mom hugged me and cried. She told me that she loved me and then told me I could not leave the house for two months, except to go to work. I told her she should increase the punishment to three months, and she laughed.

The Queen stopped by my house to welcome me back, and then told me that I would be expected to tell the story of my disobedience and capture at every Great Selecting from now on, so that my poor choices could serve as a lesson for all new fairies.

"But, your highness," I said, "that will be so embarrassing."

"Annabelle," said the Queen, "I am not interested in your embarrassment. I am interested in preventing any other fairies from being taken. You are lucky to be alive."

"I know, but . . . ."

"And," continued the Queen, obviously angry, "you are lucky no fairies were killed while rescuing you."

"Yes, your highness. I see now that you are right."

The Queen smiled. "Good. Enough of that then. I will take my leave and let you spend time with your family. I expect you back at work 48 hours from now."

"Yes, your highness," I said as I watched her leave.

About a week later, I was on fart patrol when I felt a tingling. I flew to its location and saw that it was coming from Mia's house.

I landed in a nearby tree and looked in the window. Mia was reading a book about fairies and taking notes.

I wish she still had her memories of me, I thought, as I did my "shazaam" to let her fart out.

Just then, Mia turned around and looked out the window. She looked right at me, though I was too far away for her to be able to see me.

As she stared at me, a strange look flashed across her face. Then, she looked away, shook her head and smiled to herself.

I smiled too because I knew then that she remembered me, at least in some small way, she remembered me.

The End

About the Author

I, M.T. Lott, being more or less of sound mind and body, thank you for reading this book.

There is little to say about me other than I love to write even more than I love eating Mexican food, but less than I love to surf. We all need our priorities in life.

If you enjoyed this book, I would be honored if you would **leave a review** or *recommend it to your family and friends*. And, don't forget to stop by **MTLottBooks.com** for updates on when my next book will be published.

Be sure to check out my other books, including these coloring books:

Made in the USA
Middletown, DE
11 July 2021